fearfully and wonderfully made

written by Susan E. Moody
illustrated by Bobbi Johnson and Susan E. Moody

Copyright ©2011

Kalos Books, LLC

Havre de Grace, Maryland

ISBN 978-0-9846165-1-0

Copyright © 2011 by Susan E. Moody
Published and distributed by Kalos Books, LLC, www.kalosbooks.com
Written by Susan E. Moody ~ Illustrated by Bobbi Johnson and Susan E. Moody
ISBN 978-0-9846165-1-0
www.fearfullyandwonderfullymade.me

Dedications

We dedicate this book:

To Jesus Christ, who is our Lord and Savior. His love is what gives us the words and the art that we use to tell others about how much He loves them. Without Him, life would have no meaning. Thank you Lord for making us in your image and for buying us back. We love you!

To Merci, Tevin, Ryanne, Linea, Elizabeth, Noah, Chelsea, and Jared - the best bunch of nieces and nephews a couple of aunts could have! Don't ever forget how very much we love you!

To Heidi, our friend and honorary sister. You are funny and smart and loving and beautiful, and we couldn't love you any more if we tried! Never forget that you are fearfully and wonderfully made by God Himself!

OUR GREAT THANKS to all the people who have believed in us and waited with us as we have labored over this project. Your support and encouragement have meant the world! We love you!

Way back at the start,
Before there was time,
The God of the Universe
Had you in mind.
So He set about working
To bring you to be,
And He did a great job!
It's so easy to see!

From the top of your head
To the tip of your toes;

From the shape of your eyes
To the tilt of your nose,

To the skin on your body
Whatever the shade –

You are

awesomely
awesomely
awesomely
awesomely
awesomely
awesomely
awesomely

fearfully, wonderfully made!

God made you on purpose.
You aren't some mistake!
He worked and He toiled
A great you to make.
He picked out your height,
Your shape and your size.
He molded your nose
And He colored your eyes.

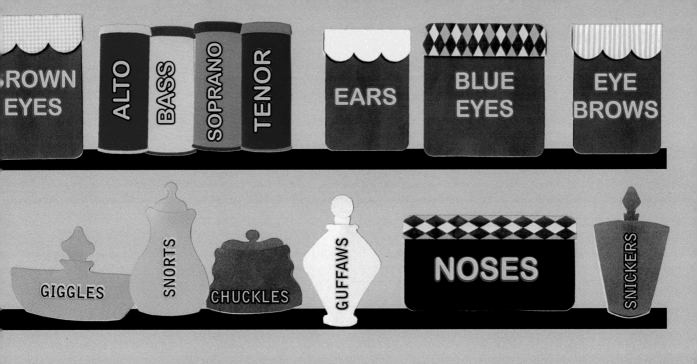

He fashioned your laugh.
Your voice He did choose.
He even determined
The size of your shoes!

There's no one like you.
No one else
makes the grade!

A⁺ Distinguished

A⁺ Extraordinary

A⁺ Irreplacable

A⁺ One-of-a-kind

A⁺ Original

A⁺ Special

A⁺ Unique

You are

purposely

purposely

purposely

purposely

purposely

purposely

purposely

fearfully, wonderfully made!

God knew the real you
Before you came to be.

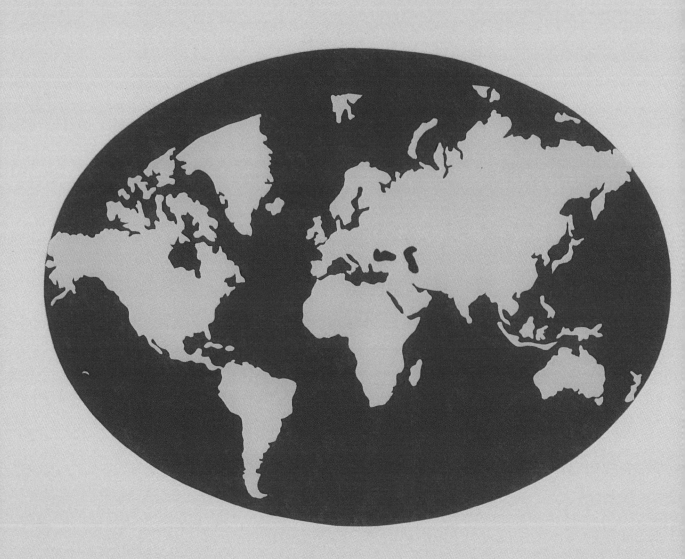

He knew where you'd live,
What you'd like on TV.

He knew what you'd eat
And what school you'd attend,

How tall you'd grow up
And who'd be your best friend.

He knew that you'd love
That one color you love;
And whether or not
You could catch
with a glove.
He knew if you'd rather
Have sunlight or shade...

'Cause you're

knowingly

knowingly

knowingly

knowingly

knowingly

knowingly

knowingly

fearfully, wonderfully made!

There's only one person could be the real you.
No other who tried it would know what to do.
No one can be found

who can sing like you sing,

There's no one with hair
Like the stuff on your head,
And no one who's read
All the books that you've read.

And no one, but no one,
Can think like you think,
Can joke like you joke,
Or can wink like you wink.

And none has you beat –
not when push comes to shove –
'Cause no one, but no one,
Can love like you love!

No one can compare –
We should throw a parade!

You are Special!

'Cause you're

specially

specially

specially

specially

specially

specially

specially

fearfully, wonderfully made!

Now there's one other thing
Most perfectly true
That should tell you for sure
You're a most special you:

The God of all gods
Knows you're worth any cost,
So He sent His son Jesus
To save what was lost.

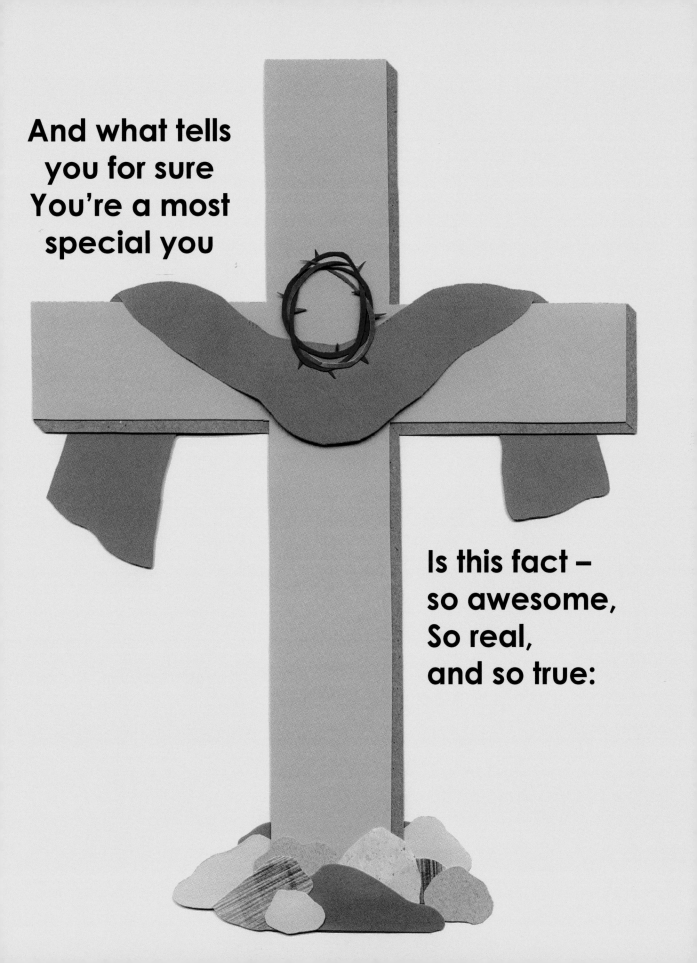

And what tells
you for sure
You're a most
special you

Is this fact –
so awesome,
So real,
and so true:

God still would have done this,
And paid what He paid,
Even if it would be
Only you that He'd save.

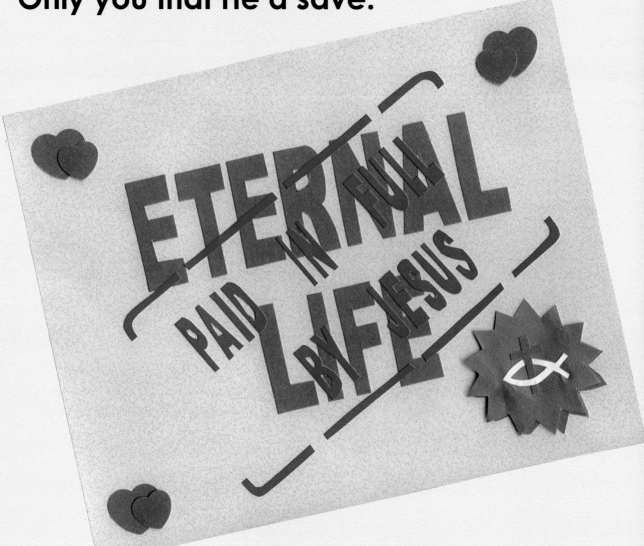

And this one simple fact
Has the argument swayed...

You are
awesomely
purposely
knowingly
specially
perfectly
fearfully
wonderfully
made!

O LORD, you have searched me and known me! You know when I sit down and when I rise up; you discern my thoughts from afar. You... are acquainted with all my ways. Even before a word is on my tongue... O LORD, you know it altogether... For you formed my inward parts; you knitted me together in my mother's womb.

I praise You, for I am fearfully and wonderfully made.

Wonderful are your works; my soul knows it very well. My frame was not hidden from you, when I was being made in secret, intricately woven in the depths of the earth. Your eyes saw my unformed substance; in your book were written, every one of them, the days that were formed for me, when as yet there were none of them...

Selections from Psalm 139 (ESV)